Periwinkle Picks The Pickle

Lauren Harrell

Illustrated by QBN Studios

Library of Congress Number: 2021920628
ISBN: 978-0-578-96417-1 (Hardcover)
ISBN: 978-1-0879-0094-0 (eBook)

www.laurenharrellauthor.com

DEDICATION

For Mom, Dad, and everyone who read this book in advance,
Thank you, it means a great *dill*.

Once a year, people from all around the Cucumber Kingdom come to the palace with pickles for the king.

Princess Periwinkle has a big task! Today, she is helping her dad pick a pickle that will be chosen for this year's winner of the Pickle of the Year contest!

Princess Periwinkle tastes all kinds of pickles, and she LOVES them!

She eats sliced pickles, big pickles, small pickles, sweet pickles, and salty pickles. She eats red pickles, yellow pickles, and even blue pickles!

She opens a new jar of pickles and pulls out a small green one. "Hey!" she hears. Princess Periwinkle gasps, dropping the pickle! Where was the voice coming from? She didn't see anyone else!

"Excuse me!" Princess Periwinkle looks down and realizes the pickle is talking! "You can talk!" Princess Periwinkle says. She had never seen a pickle do that before! "Why, of course I can talk!" the pickle says. "And I can dance too!" He taps his little green shoes with a *click, click, click.*

"My name is Peter Pickle," he says, looking back to Princess Periwinkle, whose mouth is wide open in surprise! "I would like to try out for Pickle of The Year!"

"Try out? We aren't holding auditions!" Princess Periwinkle giggles. "It's a tasting contest!"
"Well, you can't eat me!" says Peter Pickle, jumping in front of Princess Periwinkle. "Besides, I'm the smallest one in the jar and the sourest one of all! You don't want to eat the world's sourest pickle, do you?"

Princess Periwinkle thought for a moment. She could eat a sour pickle, but she didn't want to eat a live pickle! She did not like that idea at all!

"But how do you win the contest if you're not eaten?"
Princess Periwinkle wonders. Peter Pickle chuckles.
"Don't worry, Princess, I can show the king my many
talents!" Princess Periwinkle is curious! "What other
talents do you have?"

"I have many!" Peter Pickle says. "I can sing, hold tiny things, wear many hats, tell you lots of facts, do a handstand, and tie my shoes with one hand!

I can dance, wear pants, and help you water your plants!
I can make you laugh till your belly aches, fix anything
that breaks, and even bake a chocolate cake!'

Princess Periwinkle is impressed! This pickle is little, but
she's amazed by his many talents!

"Periwinkle, who are you talking to?" The king asks, munching on a humongous pickle. "This is Peter Pickle!" says Princess Periwinkle, pointing to the little green pickle.

"Hello, Your Majesty," Peter Pickle gives a perfect bow. "Wow! A talking pickle?" says the king. "He's certainly a very small pickle. What brings you here to the Cucumber Kingdom, Peter Pickle?"

"I'm auditioning for Pickle of the Year!" says Peter Pickle, tapping his shoes with a *click, click, click*. "I'm the smallest, sourest pickle you'll ever see!" he says. "But that doesn't stop me! Even the smallest creatures can do big things, like winning the Pickle of the Year contest!"

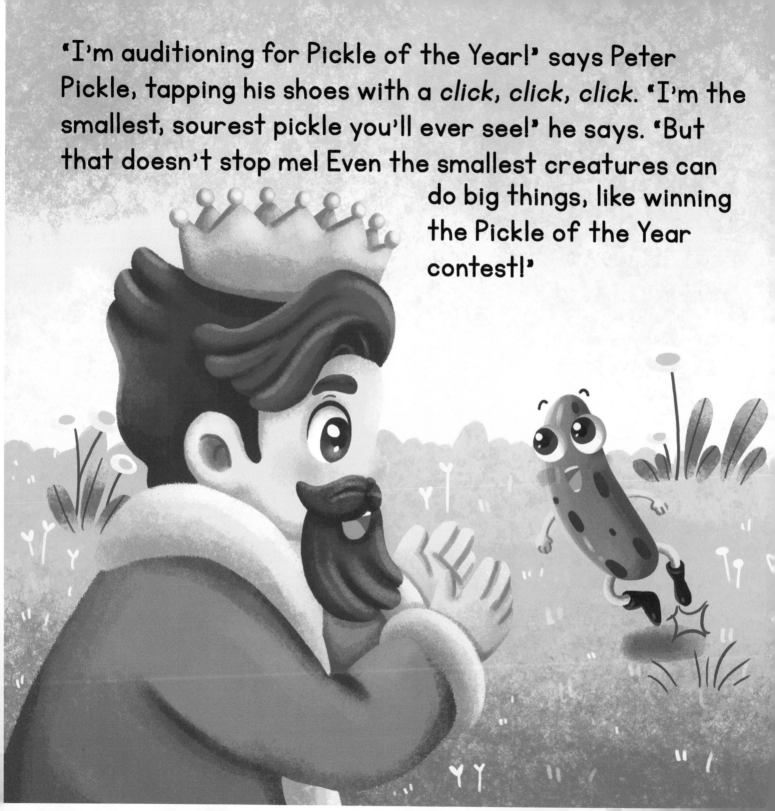

'I've never seen anything like this!' says the king. 'Is this who you'd like to pick for this year's winner, Periwinkle?'

"I know this is a pickle tasting contest," the princess says. "I really like Peter Pickle because he can sing, hold many tiny things, wear many hats, tell you lots of facts, do a handstand, and tie his shoes with one hand!

He can dance, wear pants, and help you water your plants! He can make you laugh till your belly aches, fix anything that breaks, and even bake a chocolate cake!"

The king nods. "I'm going to let you decide."

"I really like that Peter Pickle is unlike anything we've ever seen before in this contest," Princess Periwinkle continues. "One day, when I'm queen, I want every pickle to have the chance to be in our Pickle of the Year contest, even the smallest ones!"

"From here on, I declare that all pickles are welcome to participate in our contest!" says the king. "In that case, I choose Peter Pickle!" says Princess Periwinkle, pointing to Peter Pickle.

"Princess Periwinkle has picked the pickle! Let the Pickle Parade begin!" the king proclaims, and everyone cheers in celebration.

Princess Periwinkle has had the best day – because SHE got to pick the Pickle of the Year! It's the best Pickle Party that the kingdom has ever had!

AUTHOR BIO

Lauren Harrell is the author of *Periwinkle Picks the Pickle*. She currently works in marketing and volunteers for several organizations in the Houston area. She enjoys working with and being around children, and is a member of the Society of Children's Book Writers and Illustrators in Houston. When she's not writing, she's playing with her bichon frise Lucy, eating lots of pickles, or learning something new!

Lauren would like to thank her parents and everyone who read this book in advance for their encouragement and support!

CPSIA information can be obtained
at www.ICGtesting.com
Printed in the USA
LVHW071618051221
705342LV00008B/167